For Blaire and Whitney.

You're BRAVE,
You're STRONG,
You're CONFIDENT!

Alexa was sitting in the back seat, quietly looking out the window. She was feeling anxious because once again, she was moving to a new town where she didn't know anyone.

Written by J.T. and Kate Kerns
Illustrated by Remi Bryant

ISBN: 979-8-9874056-2-8 Paperback Edition
ISBN: 979-8-9874056-1-1 Hardback Edition
ISBN: 979-8-9874056-0-4 Ebook Edition

Published by Kerns Publishing
Coronado, California USA

For more information, please visit
www.kernspublishing.com

Across town, Vivian was at the park with her friends, Brooke and Emmy. The girls were playing tag, hide and seek, and their favorite game of all, sea creatures!

The next morning, Alexa sat quietly on her kitchen chair. Her mom was spreading the last bit of peanut butter on her peanut butter and banana sandwich.

Her mom looked up and said, "I can tell you're feeling nervous, sweetie. What do we tell ourselves when we're feeling nervous?"

Alexa said, "I know, I know ... I'm brave, I'm strong, I'm confident."

Her mom responded, "That's right! You have the power to make new friends, just like you've done every time we've moved." Then her mom said, "I have an idea. Let's go to the park after school today." That sounded good to Alexa.

A few blocks away, Vivian was sitting on her usual stool in the kitchen. While her mom put the last slice of banana on her peanut butter and banana sandwich, Vivian looked up and said, "School is so boring. It's the same old thing every day."

Her mom smiled and responded, "Well, my love, I got an email from Mrs. Zarston saying there would be a new kid in class today. Maybe you could make a new friend!" Meeting new people made Vivian nervous. It's hard to talk to someone you don't know. Besides, she already had friends.

Alexa slowly walked into her new classroom. She looked around the room and saw each of her new classmates laughing and playing together. She wondered to herself, "How am I ever going to make new friends if everyone is already friends with each other?"

A few minutes later, Vivian walked in and put her backpack on her assigned hook. The classroom was filled with the usual sounds of laughter and play. As Vivian turned around, she noticed something was different. She saw someone she didn't recognize sitting at her shared desk.

Vivian tentatively approached the desk. Mrs. Zarston walked over and said, "Good morning, Vivian. This is Alexa. She's new to our school and will be your desk buddy. Please make her feel welcome."

Vivian wasn't exactly sure how to make someone feel welcome. She couldn't think of anything to say, so she just smiled instead. She thought to herself, "Why am I the one who has to sit next to the new person?"

At lunch, Vivian sat down next to her friends and got her sandwich from her lunch box. She took a bite, looked at the next table, and noticed Alexa holding a similar looking sandwich.

She walked over and asked, "What kind of sandwich is that?" Alexa looked down at her sandwich and slowly looked back up saying, "Um...it's...peanut butter and banana."

Vivian's eyes opened wide and said, "No way! That's what I have too!" Both girls smiled and went back to their lunches.

After school, Vivian and her mom went to the park. She spotted her friends, and they quickly continued their game of sea creatures.

As Vivian was circling the slide, with her finger on top of her head like a narwhal tusk, she noticed Alexa sitting on the park bench with her mom.

At the same time, Alexa looked over and saw Vivian playing with the same girls from class. Her mom saw her staring and said, "Do those girls look familiar?"

"Did you meet them at school today?" Alexa looked down at her shoes and said, "Yeah, they're in my class." Mom said, "Well, why don't you go over and say hi, and see if they want to play?"

Alexa responded, "I don't know...They're already friends and might not want a new one." Mom pulled Alexa in close and said, "Perhaps, but I've been in their shoes before, and you know, new people can make the game even more fun." Her mom added, "Everyone feels nervous meeting someone new. I bet that includes your classmates."

Her mom continued, "What do we tell ourselves when we're feeling nervous?" Alexa looked up and said, "I'm brave. I'm strong. I'm confident!" Her mom gave her a wink and nudged her off the bench.

Alexa started walking towards the girls. Her legs felt like they weighed a hundred pounds each, and she could feel her hands getting clammy. As she approached, she repeated to herself, "I'm brave. I'm strong. I'm confident!"

Before she knew it, she was standing in front of the girls. Taking a deep breath, she said, "Hi Vivian. Remember me?"

Vivian smiled and said, "Of course!"

"You like peanut butter and banana sandwiches too!" Alexa smiled back and said, "Yeah, my dad introduced them to me when I was little. He's kind of weird."

Vivian giggled and said, "I thought I was the only one with a weird dad!"

The fact that they both had weird dads relaxed Alexa and made her more comfortable.

Remembering what her mom said, she asked, "It looks like you're playing sea creatures. Can I play too?"

Vivian responded, "Sure! Brooke is a megalodon, and Emmy is a giant squid."

The four girls ran off playing sea creatures, laughing and giggling like friends do, while both moms smiled.

About the Authors

J.T. and Kate Kerns are a married writing team living in Coronado, California with their two daughters. After years in the corporate world, they both transitioned to entrepreneurship, which led to the family moving five times in six years. During this time, they found storytelling was a great way to teach and share life lessons with their daughters. Upon moving to Coronado, with its vibrant military community and many who share similar experiences, they felt compelled to share their stories.

Both J.T. and Kate are avid world travelers, but equally enjoy spending time at their local beach and riding bikes around the island with their girls.